BIOGRAPHIES

JAMES MADISON

by Laura K. Murray

PEBBLE
a capstone imprint

Pebble Explore is published by Pebble, an imprint of Capstone.
1710 Roe Crest Drive
North Mankato, Minnesota 56003
www.capstonepub.com

Library of Congress Cataloging-in-Publication data is available on the Library of Congress website.
ISBN 978-1-9771-2331-2 (library binding)
ISBN 978-1-9771-2656-6 (paperback)
ISBN 978-1-9771-2339-8 (ebook pdf)

Summary: Describes the early life, challenges, and major accomplishments of James Madison, the fourth president of the United States of America.

Image Credits
Bridgeman Images: Wood Ronsaville Harlin, Inc. USA, 12; Getty Images: Bettmann, 18, GraphicaArtis, 19, The Washington Post/Michael S. Williamson, 25, VCG/Corbis/Geoffrey Clements, 23; iStockphoto: traveler1116, 16, 29; Library of Congress: 11, 15; Line of Battle Enterprise: 5; National Gallery of Art: Ailsa Mellon Bruce Fund, 27; Newscom: Everett Collection, cover, 1; North Wind Picture Archives: 17, Gerry Embleton, 21; Shutterstock: Curly Pat (geometric background), cover, back cover, 2, 29, DavidNNP, 26, Everett Historical, 9, 13, Morphart Creation, 22; The New York Public Library: 7, 8; Wikimedia: Princeton University Art Museum, 20

Editorial Credits
Editor: Erika L. Shores; Designer: Elyse White; Media Researcher: Svetlana Zhurkin; Production Specialist: Spencer Rosio

All internet sites appearing in back matter were available and accurate when this book was sent to press.

Printed in the United States
PO117

Table of Contents

Words in **bold** are in the glossary.

Who Was James Madison?

James Madison was the fourth leader, or **president**, of the United States. He helped plan the new country's **government**. He wanted the American people to have **rights**. He helped the states work together.

James came up with many ideas in the **U.S. Constitution**. This document is still important today. It gives rights to the American people. It says what the government can and cannot do. James helped make the country we know today.

Growing Up James

James Madison was born about 270 years ago on March 16, 1751. He was born in Port Conway, Virginia. At that time, Virginia was a **colony** ruled by the British.

James was the oldest of 12 children. The Madisons were rich. When James was a boy, they moved to a large farm. It was called Montpelier. **Enslaved** people built the house. They were forced to work the lands and grow tobacco.

Montpelier

Young James liked to read and learn. From age 11 to 16, he lived away from home at **boarding school**. He did well in math, science, and languages. Then he went to college in New Jersey.

The college James went to later became Princeton University.

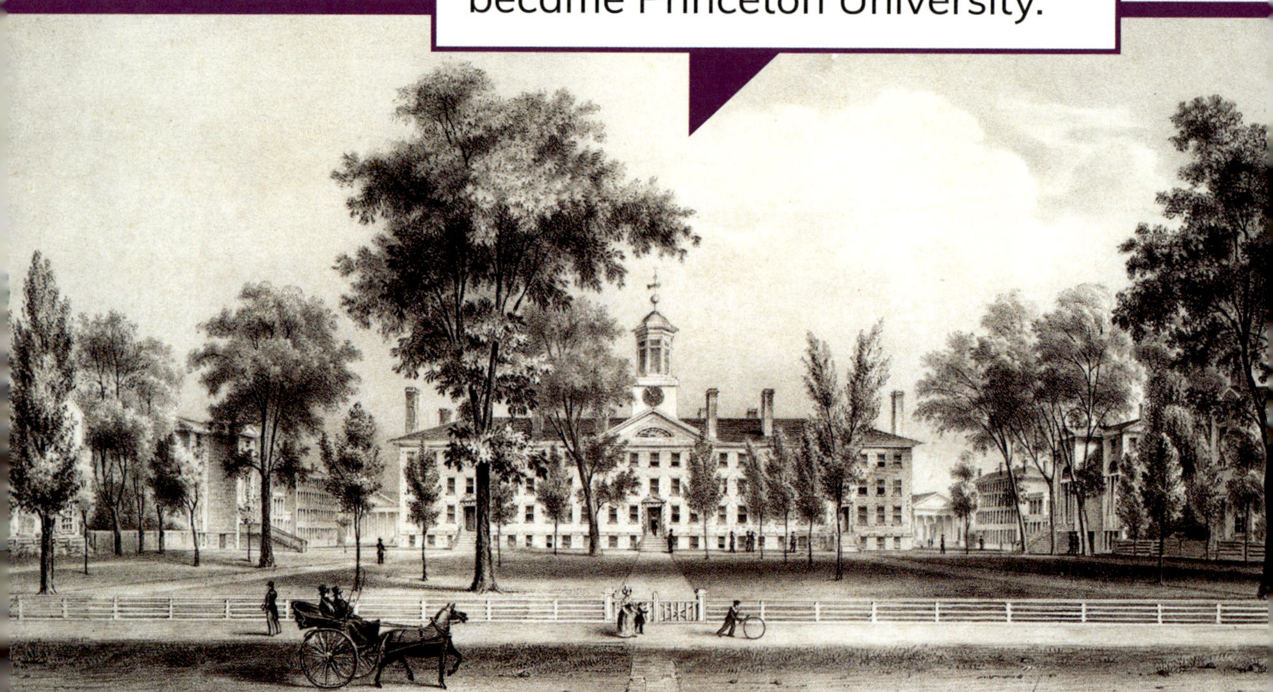

Thomas Jefferson

After college, James wanted to work in government. In 1776, James won a spot in Virginia government. He was 25. There James met Thomas Jefferson. They became friends for life. Thomas would also become a U.S. president.

A Young Leader

James and other leaders wanted American colonies to cut ties with the British. During the **Revolutionary War** (1775–1783), the Americans fought to be their own country.

In 1780, James became the youngest person in the **Continental Congress**. He was only 29 years old. He served for three years.

James in 1783

The American people won the war. But the states were not working together. James wanted a strong country. In 1787, he wrote a plan for a new government. It was called the Virginia Plan.

In 1787, state leaders used James's plan. They wrote the U.S. Constitution. James and other leaders signed it on September 17, 1787. But the states still needed to agree to it. James, Alexander Hamilton, and John Jay wrote papers saying why others should agree to the Constitution.

the Bill of Rights

In 1788, the Constitution became the law of the land. Three years later, James helped write the Bill of Rights. It said what freedoms Americans had.

The Madisons at Home

In 1794, James met Dolley Payne Todd in Philadelphia. James and Dolley were married the same year. Dolley's first husband had died. James became father to Dolley's son, John. James was shy. But Dolley was popular. She loved meeting new people.

In 1801, James's father died. James took over Montpelier at age 50. James's mother also lived there. More than 100 enslaved people worked there.

Dolley Madison

James was quiet, smart, and worked hard. He enjoyed reading in other languages. Sometimes he played chess. He liked going for walks. He rode his horse too. Dolley kept the family busy with parties.

Around 1790, James and Thomas Jefferson started a new **political party**. People in the group shared the same ideas about government.

People danced at parties in the 1700s.

The Fourth President

James was in the U.S. House of Representatives. This was one part of government that helped make laws. He served from 1789 to 1797. In 1801, President Thomas Jefferson made James his secretary of state. James and his family moved to Washington, D.C.

James and Thomas Jefferson

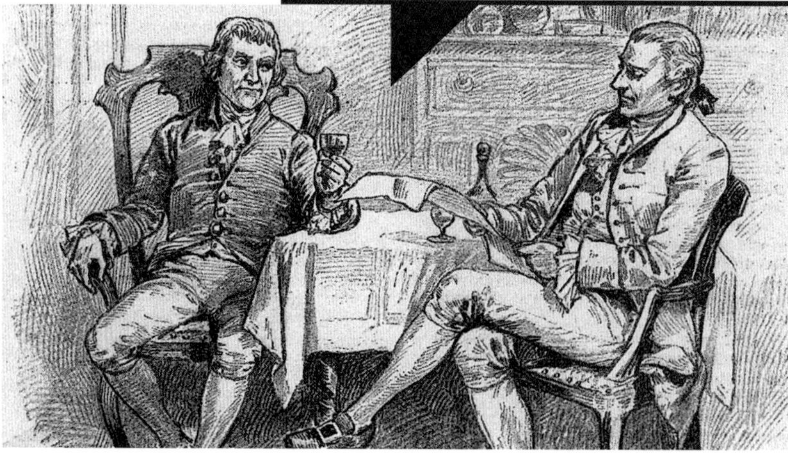

a map of the Louisiana Purchase

In his new job, James worked with other countries. In 1803, he helped make a deal with France. It was called the Louisiana Purchase. It nearly doubled the size of the United States.

In 1808, James ran for president. He won! James became the fourth U.S. president at age 57. During the War of 1812, the U.S. fought the British. The British burned down much of Washington, D.C. They even burned the White House. Dolley and an enslaved man named Paul Jennings saved important items.

In 1813, James became president for a second time. As president, James helped make a U.S. bank. He also set up plans for the country's taxes and troops.

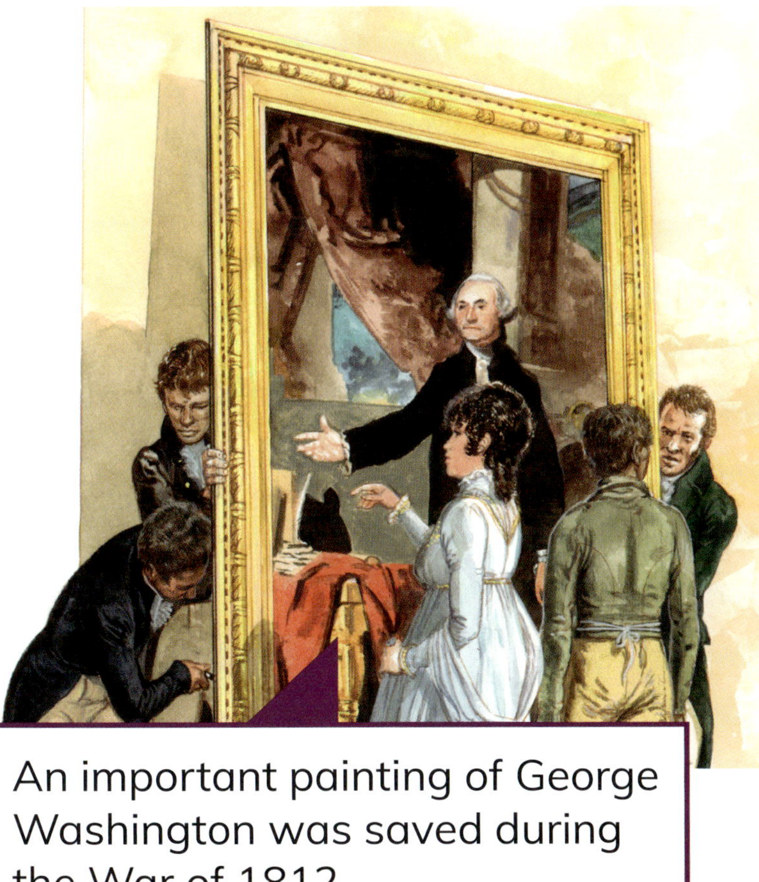

An important painting of George Washington was saved during the War of 1812.

James did not run for president again. In 1817, James and Dolley went back to Montpelier. James had changes made to the house and grounds. He thought of new ways of farming wheat and tobacco. He wrote papers on government. In 1826, he became the leader of the University of Virginia.

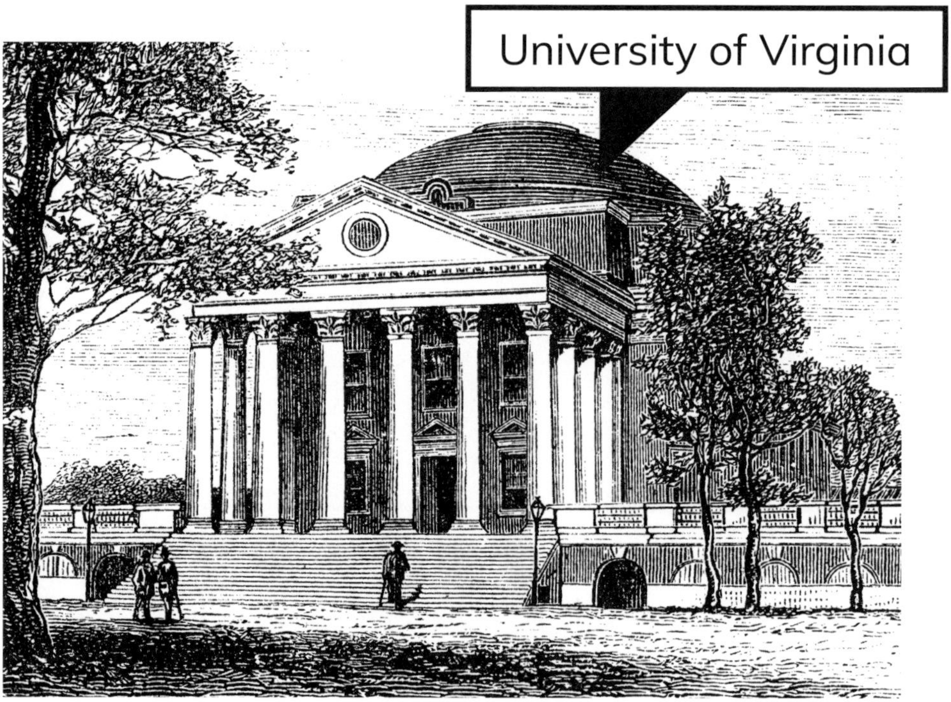

James died on June 28, 1836, at his home. He was 85 years old. He was buried at Montpelier.

Remembering Madison

Today, people can visit places to learn about James's life. Each year, more than 125,000 people go to Montpelier. People see the home, grounds, and a museum. They learn about James, his family, and the enslaved people who had to work at Montpelier.

Many places are named for James. His name is on schools, buildings, and ships. The city of Madison, Wisconsin, is named for him. Madison Square Garden is in New York City. It is known for holding big events.

Students visiting Montpelier

In Washington, D.C., people see the Constitution and the Bill of Rights. They learn about James's beliefs in freedom. The James Madison Memorial Building is part of the Library of Congress.

The James Madison Memorial Building is in Washington, D.C.

James Madison was a quiet but powerful leader. He will always be known as the Father of the Constitution. But he always said he did not do it alone. He knew that the United States was made by many people working together.

Important Dates

March 16, 1751	James Madison is born in Virginia.
1776	James is elected to the Virginia state government.
1780–83	James serves in the Continental Congress.
1787	James writes the Virginia Plan.
September 17, 1787	James signs the U.S. Constitution.
1791	James helps write the Bill of Rights.
1794	James marries Dolley Payne Todd.
1801	James becomes Thomas Jefferson's secretary of state.
1803	James helps make the Louisiana Purchase.
1809	James becomes the fourth president of the United States.
1813	James becomes president for a second time.
June 28, 1836	James dies at Montpelier.

Fast Facts

Name:
James Madison

Role:
fourth president of the United States

Life dates:
March 16, 1751 to June 28, 1836

Key accomplishments:
James Madison was the fourth president of the United States. He was elected two times and served during the War of 1812. His ideas were the basis for the U.S. Constitution. He also helped write the Bill of Rights.

Glossary

boarding school (BOR-ding SKOOL)—a school where students live during the school year

colony (KAH-luh-nee)—an area that has been settled by people from another country and is owned by that country

Continental Congress (kahn-tuh-nen-tuhl KAHNG-gruhs)—leaders from the 13 original American colonies who made up the American government from 1774 to 1789

enslave (en-SLAYV)—to make someone lose their freedom

government (GUHV-urn-muhnt)—the group of people who make rules and decisions for a country or state

political party (puh-LIT-uh-kuhl PAR-tee)—a group of people with the same ideas about government

president (PREZ-uh-duhnt)—the highest elected job in a class, business, or country

Revolutionary War (rev-uh-LOO-shuhn-air-ee WOR)—the American colonies' fight from 1775 to 1783 for freedom from Great Britain

right (RYT)—something that everyone should be able to do or to have and that the government shouldn't be able to take away, such as the right to speak freely

U.S. Constitution (YOO ESS kahn-stuh-TOO-shuhn)—the plan for how the U.S. government works

Read More

Britton, Arthur K. *20 Fun Facts about James Madison.* New York: Gareth Stevens Publishing, 2018.

Lusted, Marcia Amidon. *The Bill of Rights.* North Mankato, MN: Capstone Press, 2020.

Ransom, Candice. *James Madison.* Minneapolis: Cody Koala, 2019.

Internet Sites

James Madison
https://www.whitehouse.gov/about-the-white-house/presidents/james-madison/

Montpelier
https://www.montpelier.org/

U.S. Presidents: James Madison
https://millercenter.org/president/madison

Index